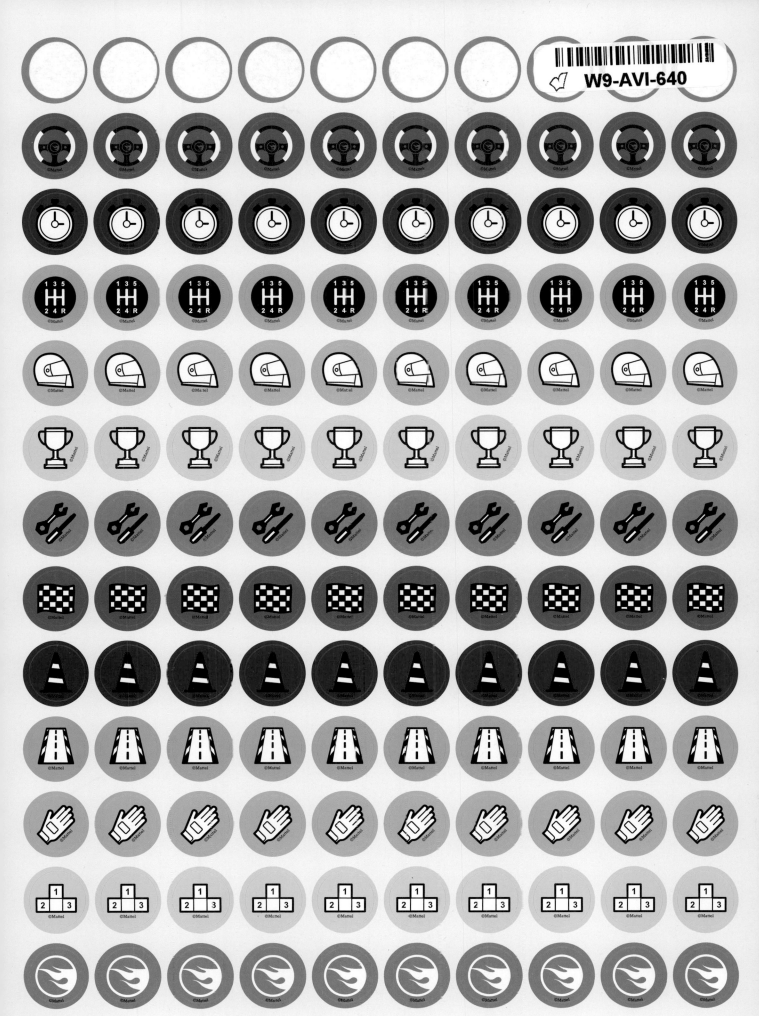

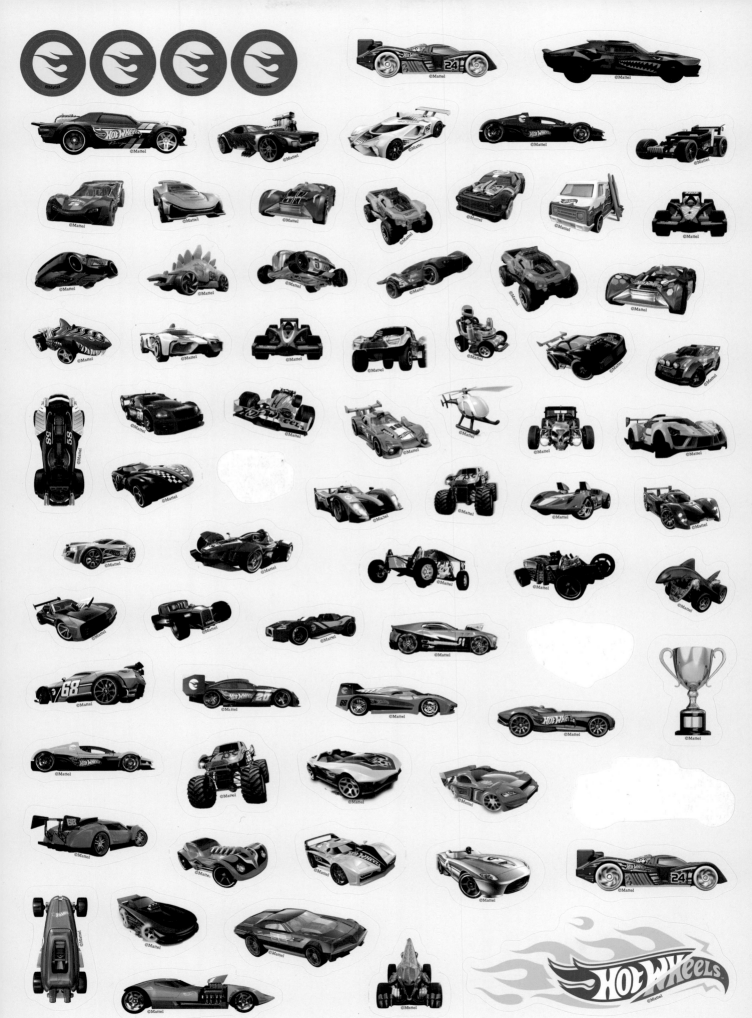

D-MUSCLE™

This all-American muscle car is built for serious asphalt burning. With a supercharged V-8, this broad-shouldered show-off is always eager to race.

TWIN MILL

You'll see double with this car's dual blown big blocks and intakes. A full-size model was displayed at auto shows and Hot Wheels™ HQ!

MUSCLE SPEEDER™

This classic muscle car has an oversized, supercharged V-8 engine. It's a supersized power force to be reckoned with!

VELOCI-RACER™

There's no backing down for this beast. It's built to chase down and catch anything in front of it.

MOD ROD

This car is a modified classic hot rod containing a powerful V-6 and a massive ram air system. This cool rod has a panoramic front windshield.

SHARK BITE™

Just when you thought it was safe, this street beast will chomp up your car! This model has sports Modified 5-Spoke (M5SP) wheels on the front so that the ferocious jaws can move!

Help the racers along the different tracks by looking for Hot Wheels™ cars and other hidden objects in the racetrack scenes. Learn more about the cars below. Which one is your favorite to win the global competition? Then, flip the page to start the race! Check out the extra Pit Stop puzzles on each track, too!

MACH SPEEDER™

Built for endurance, this mid-engine machine is powered by a twin turbo V-6 hybrid engine. The Mach Speeder™ makes a mockery of the competition!

RODGER DODGER®

With four electric motors—one for each wheel—this monster delivers tons of torque! This next-gen muscle car rockets from 0-60 mph in 1.2 seconds and tops out at 374 mph.

BLITZSPEEDER™

The Blitzspeeder™ is here, ready to cut corners and crush your track records! Don't get in its way. The last thing you may see is its oversized rear wing!

BONE SHAKER

This classic hot rod is a stripped-down Larry Wood-designed truck. With a skull grille and skeletal hands around the headlamps, it's a forbidding contestant with attitude!

RIP ROD™

Reaching top speeds upward of 125 mph, this ripper's got some kick. The fanlike exhaust tips and mask for a grille make this one racer you don't want to mess with!

NIGHT SHIFTER™

Inspired by the raw, mechanical aspects of high-performing race cars and legendary military planes, Night Shifter™ features twin turbo-chargers as well as two fuel tanks.

TRACK 1
ADRENALINE ARENA

Fasten your seatbelts and start your engines. It's time for a new adventure! Ready, set, go! Mod Rod takes an early lead!

See if you can spot all these items hidden in this scene. Place a wheel sticker next to each one you find.

PIT STOP PUZZLE

Shake, rattle, and roll! Unscramble the name of this deadly dragster!

NEBO **REASKH**

5

TRACK 2
CACTUS CANYON

Loop-de-loop through the canyon. You need courage and speed to ride this track! Veloci-Racer™ pulls ahead.

PIT STOP PUZZLE

Reveal the mystery muscle machine. Can you identify this rockin' racer and spot him in this scene?

See if you can spot all of these items hidden in this scene. Place a steering wheel sticker next to each one you find.

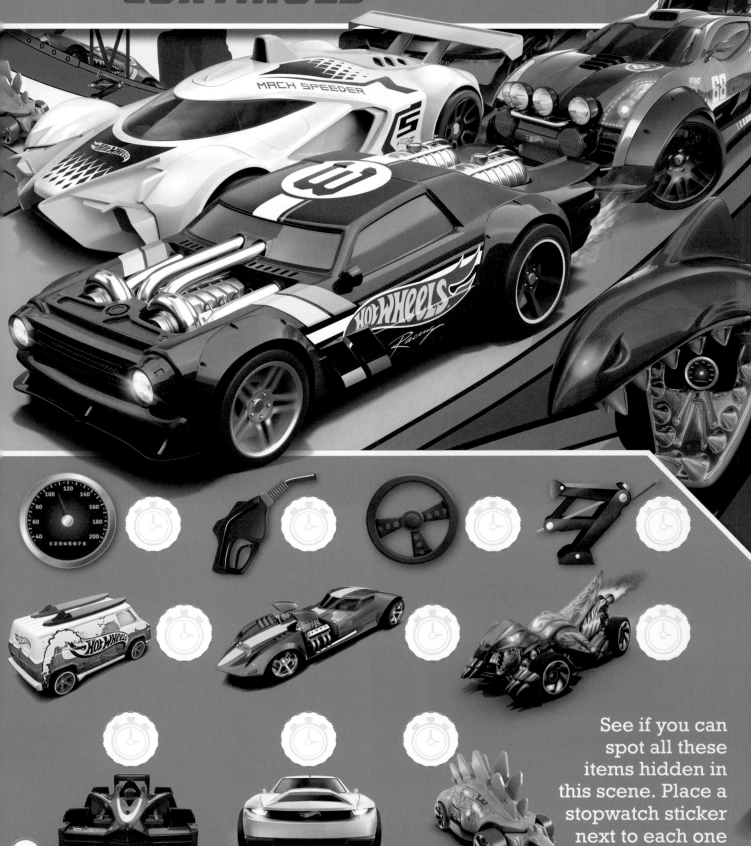

CACTUS CANYON
THE RACE CONTINUES

Night Shifter™ shows no mercy on the Spire Climb. Nice maneuver, Bone Shaker. You're unstoppable!

See if you can spot all these items hidden in this scene. Place a stopwatch sticker next to each one you find.

PIT STOP PUZZLE

Circle the letters in the maze to uncover the name of this mean machine.

TRACK 3
SKYLINE SPRINT

Mach Speeder™ gets massive air by taking the jump. This daredevil is a thrill seeker! Watch out, extreme machines—he's next level!

See if you can spot all these items hidden in this scene. Place a gear shifter sticker next to each one you find.

PIT STOP PUZZLE

Draw in the boxes so that each Hot Wheels™ badge appears only once in each row and column.

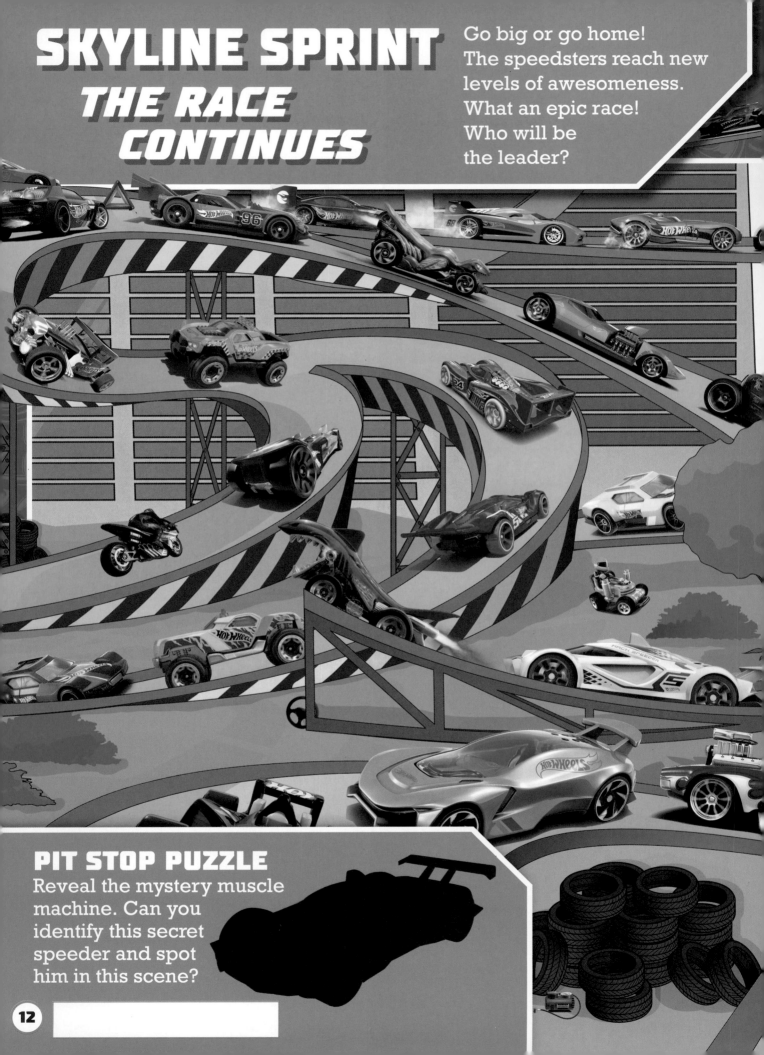

SKYLINE SPRINT
THE RACE CONTINUES

Go big or go home!
The speedsters reach new
levels of awesomeness.
What an epic race!
Who will be
the leader?

PIT STOP PUZZLE

Reveal the mystery muscle
machine. Can you
identify this secret
speeder and spot
him in this scene?

See if you can spot all of these items hidden in this scene. Place a racing helmet sticker next to each one you find.

TRACK 4
CITY CIRCUIT

Fight for pole position.
Shark Bite™ is ferocious!
He's ravenous for success
and devours the track.
Full throttle!

PIT STOP PUZZLE
Unleash the beast! Who am I?

- ENORMOUS V8 ENGINE
- RED BODYWORK
- A DRAGON OF A CAR

See if you can spot all of these items hidden in this scene. Place a trophy sticker next to each one you find.

15

TRACK 5
RAINFOREST RALLY

The superfast roadsters race along the tropical track to jungle jump. D-Muscle™ clears the canopy. What an excellent performance!

See if you can spot all these items hidden in this scene. Place a tool sticker next to each one you find.

PIT STOP PUZZLE

Can you name this prehistoric "beast" of a car?

RAINFOREST RALLY
THE RACE CONTINUES

What a display! These high-powered racers are running wild! Stay on track for a spectacular show.

See if you can spot all these items hidden in this scene. Place a flag sticker next to each one you find.

PIT STOP PUZZLE

Unscramble the letters to reveal this twin turbo speedster!

G	I	H	T	N

R	I	F	S	E	H	T

TRACK 6
SPEEDWAY STADIUM

Optimal downforce. Blitzspeeder™ breaks away from the rest. Could this be a new speed record?

PIT STOP PUZZLE
Can you name this muscle car?

See if you can spot all these items hidden in this scene. Place a cone sticker next to each one you find.

SPEEDWAY STADIUM
THE RACE CONTINUES

Twin Mill picks up the pace as the competition gets fierce. It's all or nothing as the rivals take on the speedway loop-de-loops.

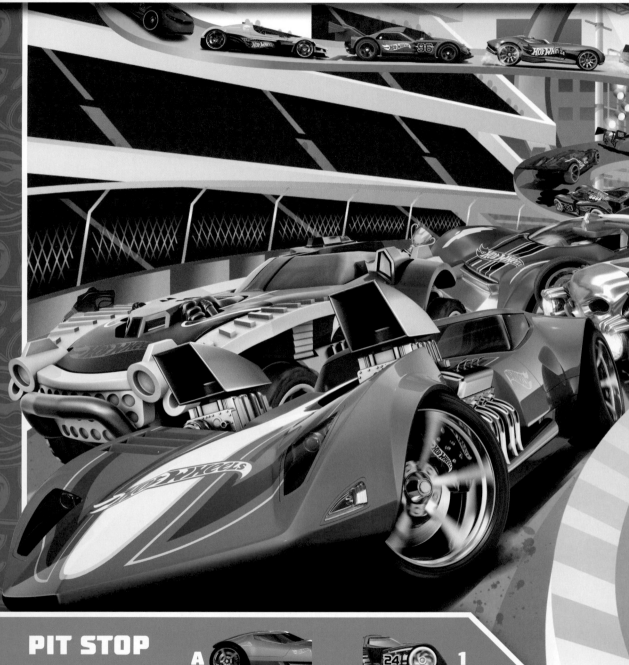

PIT STOP PUZZLE

Draw lines between the matching halves of these mean machines.

A

B

C

D

 1

 2

 3

 4

See if you can spot all of these items hidden in this scene.
Place a road sticker next to each one you find.

TRACK 7
CALAMITY CREEK

Engines are roaring and wheels are turning! Are the cars ready to take on the twists and turns through Calamity Creek?

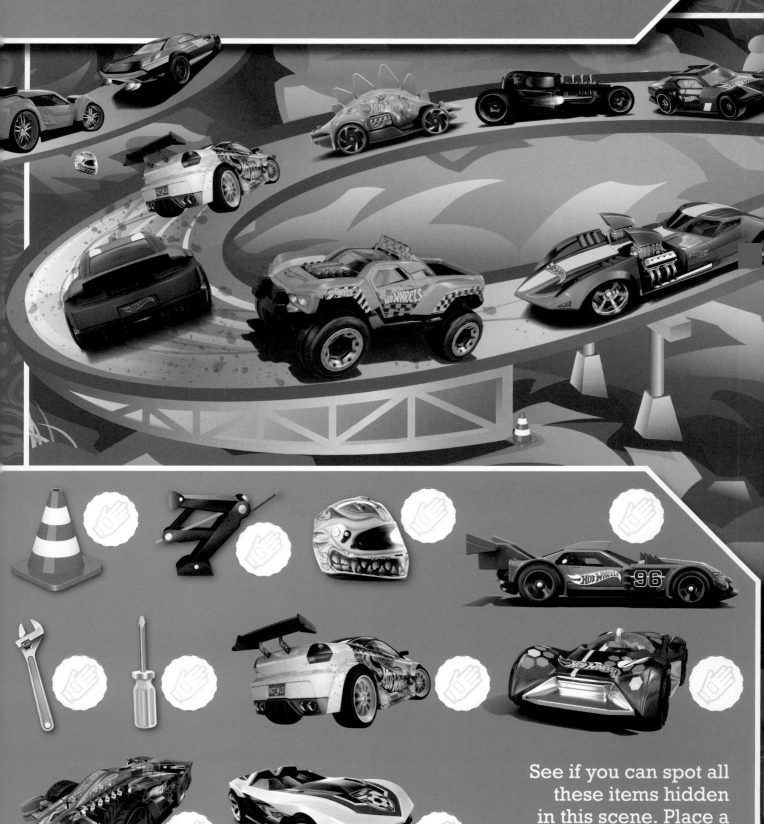

See if you can spot all these items hidden in this scene. Place a glove sticker next to each one you find.

24

PIT STOP PUZZLE

Unscramble these letters to reveal the name of this rockin' roadster!

O D M   **D O R**

CALAMITY CREEK
THE RACE CONTINUES

Rip Rod™ takes a flying leap as the competition continues. Who do you think will take the lead? It's anyone's race!

PIT STOP PUZZLE

I am named after a ferocious predator's attack.
Who am I?

See if you can spot all of these items hidden in this scene. Place a winners podium sticker next to each one you find.

TRACK 8
FEARSOME FALLS

Prepare yourself for the ultimate ride. The drivers take on the final challenge as the race reaches its climax!

See if you can spot all these items hidden in this scene. Place a flame sticker next to each one you find.

PIT STOP PUZZLE

Can you identify this super speedster and spot him in this scene?

29

PHOTO FINISH

Wow! What an awesome finish to this amazing race! The cars reach the checkered flag, but it's too close to call—it's going to be a photo finish. Who do you think is the global champion?

See if you can spot all of these items hidden in this scene. Place a purple and yellow flame sticker next to each one you find.

BONUS FIND

Now, look back through the book and see if you can find this trophy hiding in each scene!

Answers

TRACK 1: ADRENALINE ARENA (4-5)

PIT STOP PUZZLE - BONE SHAKER

TRACK 2: CACTUS CANYON (6-7)

PIT STOP PUZZLE - TWIN MILL

TRACK 2: CACTUS CANYON [CONTINUED] (8-9)

PIT STOP PUZZLE - BLITZSPEEDER™

TRACK 3: SKYLINE SPRINT (10-11)

PIT STOP PUZZLE -

TRACK 3: SKYLINE SPRINT [CONTINUED] (12-13)

PIT STOP PUZZLE - MACH SPEEDER™

TRACK 4: CITY CIRCUIT (14-15)

PIT STOP PUZZLE - RODGER DODGER®

TRACK 5: RAINFOREST RALLY (16-17)

PIT STOP PUZZLE - VELOCI-RACER™

Answers

TRACK 5: RAINFOREST RALLY (CONTINUED) (18-19)

PIT STOP PUZZLE - NIGHT SHIFTER™

TRACK 6: SPEEDWAY STADIUM (20-21)

PIT STOP PUZZLE - MUSCLE SPEEDER™

TRACK 6: SPEEDWAY STADIUM (CONTINUED) (22-23)

PIT STOP PUZZLE - A-3, B-4, C-1, D-2

TRACK 7: CALAMITY CREEK (24-25)

PIT STOP PUZZLE - MOD ROD

TRACK 7: CALAMITY CREEK (CONTINUED) (26-27)

PIT STOP PUZZLE - SHARK BITE™

TRACK 8: FEARSOME FALLS (28-29)

PIT STOP PUZZLE - RODGER DODGER®

PHOTO FINISH (30)